Over and Over

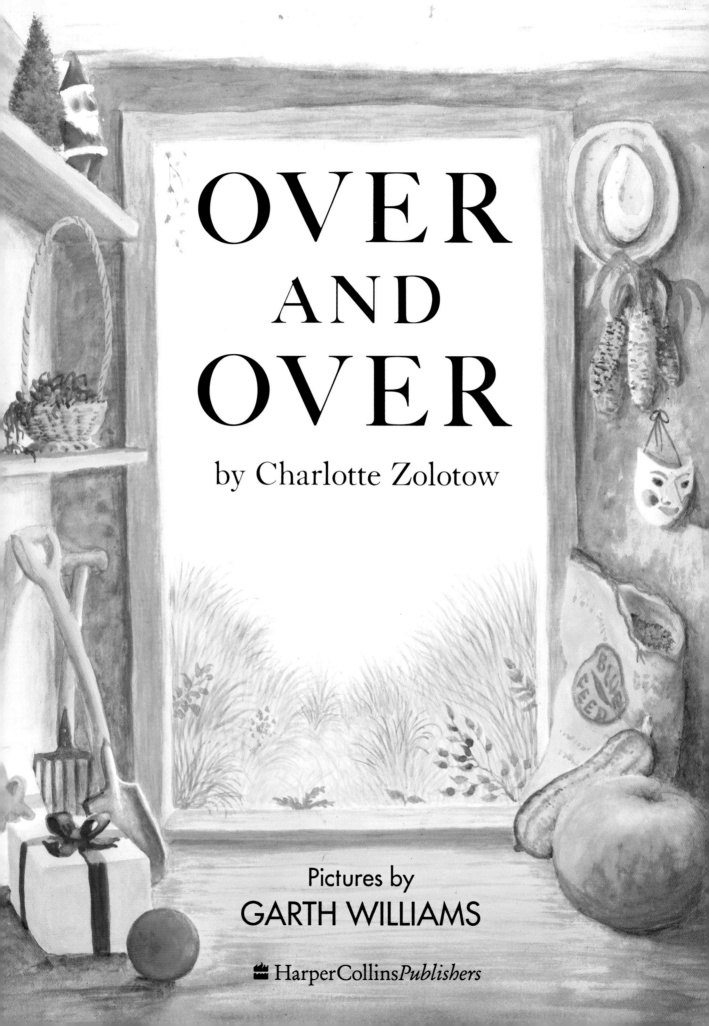

OVER
AND
OVER

by Charlotte Zolotow

Pictures by
GARTH WILLIAMS

HarperCollins*Publishers*

Library of Congress Cataloging-in-Publication Data
Zolotow, Charlotte, 1915–
   Over and over.
   Summary: A little girl and her mother observe the
passage of the seasons as they celebrate the year's
holidays, beginning with Christmas and ending after
Thanksgiving with a birthday wish that the cycle begin
all over again
ISBN 0-06-026955-3. — ISBN 0-06-026956-1 (lib.
bdg.)
ISBN 0-06-443415-X (pbk.)
   [1. Holidays—Fiction.   2. Seasons—Fiction.]
   I. Williams, Garth, ill.   II. Title.
PZ7.Z77Ov   1987
[E]   86-29487

To my dear friend and editor,
Ursula Nordstrom

Once there was a little girl who didn't understand about time. She was so little that she didn't know about Monday, Tuesday, Wednesday, Thursday, Friday, Saturday, Sunday. She certainly didn't know about January, February, March, April, May, June, July, August, September, October, November, December. She was so little she didn't even know summer, winter, autumn, spring.

What she did know about was all mixed together. She remembered a crocus once, but she didn't know when. She remembered a snowman and a pumpkin, and a Christmas tree, and a birthday cake, a Thanksgiving dinner and valentines. But they were all mixed up in her mind.

So one morning when she woke up and looked out of the window she was very excited.

"See! Come! See what happened!" she called.

The garden was white!

"That's snow," her mother said.

The little girl stared. The snow almost made her remember something else. Something nice. But she couldn't remember exactly what. She only half-remembered.

What comes next?" she asked.

"Christmas," said her mother. And one day soon after, it was! There was holly on the mantel with shiny pointed leaves and bright red berries. There was a Christmas tree in the corner of the room. There were red packages and white packages and green packages and everyone opened everything. The floor was covered with tissue paper and with little cards saying "Merry Christmas."

The little girl loved Christmas. But she half-remembered something else.

What comes next?" she asked that night.

"Valentine's Day comes next," said her mother.

The little girl woke up and went to sleep many times, and it snowed and the wind blew. Then one day she woke up and the breakfast table was full of little envelopes for her.

"For me?" she asked.

"For you," her mother said.

The little girl opened the envelopes. There were red hearts with white lace, and lace squares with purple violets. There were roses with stems and little poems. There were bright red hearts that said "I love you," and all of them said "Happy Valentine's Day!"

"For me?" said the little girl.

"For you," said her mother. And the little girl was very happy, though she half-remembered something else.

What comes next now?" she asked.

"Easter," said her mother.

The little girl waited. She woke up many mornings and went for many walks and had many baths. Then one morning the air was soft and warm and the birds were singing outside and the little girl went downstairs, and there was a big basket full of shiny green paper grass and a big chocolate egg with white icing on it. And there were some little fuzzy yellow chicks and one little bunny who played music when she wound him.

"I like Easter," the little girl said. But that night she asked, "What comes next?"

Vacation comes next," said her mother smiling. "We are going to the seashore."

The weather grew warmer and warmer. The crocus the little girl remembered bloomed again, the leaves came out on all the trees, the grass was thick and green, and it was hot. One day the little girl's family got into the car with many suitcases and off they drove to the seashore.

There was a little house right on the beach, and the little girl found snail shells and clam shells and lovely shiny oyster shells. Every day she went swimming in the cool water. Every night she heard the waves pounding up and away from the sand when she went to sleep. But one day vacation was over and the mother and father and little girl got in their car and drove home.

The house looked bigger than the little girl remembered and all her toys seemed like new. The leaves began to turn red and yellow and brown and the chrysanthemums bloomed. The little girl half-remembered something again.

W hat comes now?" she asked.

"Halloween," said her mother. The little girl and her mother drove to the store and bought a big basket of apples and a jug of apple cider and some fresh warm doughnuts and a big pumpkin that they took home and scooped out. The little girl watched her mother carve a big happy smile and a little triangular nose and two triangular eyes in the pumpkin.

That night the little girl stood by the door and every time the bell rang she asked the ghosts and witches and tigers and tramps and devils who came, "What's your name?"

But all they said was, "Trick or treat?"

And the little girl handed them their treat of doughnuts and apples and said, "Happy Halloween," when they went away.

What comes next?" she asked her mother the next day.

"Thanksgiving," her mother said. The little girl woke up one day to a delicious roasting smell and the fragrance of pies. That afternoon her grandmother and grandfather and uncles and aunts all came to her house for dinner and afterward they sat in front of the fire and cracked open walnuts and ate the soft sweet kernels.

D oes anything come now?" the little girl asked that night.

"Oh, yes," said her mother. "The next thing that comes is a very special day. Your birthday!"

And, sure enough, one day the little girl woke up from her nap and her mother dressed her in her party shoes and her party dress and combed her hair and washed her face. When she came downstairs, the little girl saw the house was full of balloons. There were red balloons, pink balloons, white balloons, blue balloons, and the table was set with a blue tablecloth and pink baskets of nuts and blue and pink flowers and funny pink and blue hats.

The doorbell began to ring and the little girl's friends kept coming with presents. When the presents were all opened and everyone had played ring-around-a-rosy, they all sat down at the table. Then the little girl's mother brought in a cake with pink candles. Everyone sang "Happy Birthday to You."

Then the little girl made a wish and blew out the candles.

"What did you wish?" everyone asked her.

"I wished for it all to happen again," the little girl said.

And of course, over and
over, year after year, it did.

THE END